FIVE HUNDRED MILES

KEVIN BROOKS

First published in 2016 in Great Britain by
Barrington Stoke Ltd
18 Walker Street, Edinburgh, EH3 7LP

www.barringtonstoke.co.uk

A CIP catalogue record for this book is
available from the British Library upon
request

ISBN: 978-1-78112-540-3

Printed in China by Leo

CONTENTS

CHAPTER 1
SUNDAY MORNING

Imagine a back street outside a breaker's yard in East London on a damp October morning. The air is spun with a mist of rain, the skies are low, the gutters are glazed with petrol rainbows. For the moment, all is still. The streets are empty. Nothing moves. Nothing whispers.

Then, with a dull clack of metal, the gates of the yard creak open and two boys walk out into the silent rain. They pause for a moment, both of them pull up their collars, then they shrug their shoulders and walk up the street. Under their feet, the petrol rainbows shimmer and break in the rain.

Side by side, step by step, with their hands in their pockets and their eyes fixed hard to the ground, the two boys move along the street and away into the morning gloom. They walk as they always walk – with the steady silence of brothers. This is their way.

They have no need to talk, for there's nothing new to say, and they have no need to look where they are going, for this is their world. The back-street world. Its shadowed lands are mapped in their hearts. The sooty railway bridges and the brick walls tagged with graffiti, the arched tunnels of scrap metal and old car batteries, the green canals, the flat grey sky. They know these things as well as they know themselves. The purple weeds and torn posters and sagging heaps of sand. The red-brick flats with metal bars on the windows. The grey and white gusts of flapping pigeons. The concrete deserts. The wastelands.

They know it all.

To Cole and Ruben, it's nowhere.

Everywhere.

And here they are, walking it together, alone with their thoughts.

Ruben is the younger of the two. He's lost in a dream of his own making, a vision of high mountains and eagles swooping in a wide-open sky ...

Cole is thinking of his sister. He isn't aware that he's thinking of her, because he thinks of her every day, and these thoughts have become automatic. Like breathing. Like walking. Like living. When he thinks about Rachel, he thinks with the core of his mind. It thinks for him. It searches the darkness, trying to find her, trying to picture her face – her eyes, her chestnut hair, the way she'd smile and light up the world ... but that was all a long time ago, too far away, and the pictures aren't there any more.

The only thing that comes to his mind now is an empty hole, a shadow, a person he doesn't know. A girl with sunken eyes and scarred skin and the husk of a broken smile ...

Cole puts his hand to his head and wipes the rain from his eyes.

Somewhere far away, a bell rings out. As the mournful sound dies in the air, Cole stops walking and listens. Ruben stops beside him and listens with him. It's quiet for a moment, then a thin whistle of city wind rattles the street, scraping the air like the breath of a dying man. Cole lets it ride, listening instead to the other world, the real world – the sound of dogs barking, music playing, a brief burst of raised voices. Not too far away, the wail of a siren pulses through the streets.

"What's the matter, Cole?" Ruben asks.

Cole looks at him, and wonders for a second how he'd feel if Ruben wasn't his brother. If the boy beside him was a stranger, what would he think of that unworldly face, that bulky black coat, that wiry explosion of hair? What would he think of those ageless blue eyes?

Would he think – as he often did – that
this 14-year-old boy knows nothing at
all and everything there is to know, and
doesn't care which is which?

"Cole?" Ruben says. "What is it?"

"Nothing." Cole touches his brother's
arm. "Come on, let's go."

They move on through the rain.

It's nine o'clock.

Sunday morning.

CHAPTER 2
THE LIVE AND LET LIVE

The pub at the end of the street – the Live and Let Live – is an unwelcoming building of grey-washed brick and dirty windows. There's a main door on the High Street, back-street doors on either side, and a broad alley that runs along the building at the back. The alley walls are black with age and topped with upturned nails and shards of broken glass. At the front of the pub, a weather-worn sign hangs over the door on two creaking chains. It shows a badly painted lion lying down with an equally badly painted lamb.

Cole and Ruben enter the pub by one of the side doors, then they move on through another door into a dimly lit corridor. Their clothes are damp and their hair is wet. While Ruben wrinkles his nose and shakes the rain from his coat, Cole just stands there. He looks around, takes it all in. The stained lino, the payphones on the wall, the corkboards pinned with business cards for taxi firms and escort agencies, the hand-written cards advertising flats for rent and cheap hotels.

Models Wanted

Cash Paid For Clean Cars

The air smells bad.

Cole takes a folded brown envelope from his back pocket. The top half is dark with rain, and the edges are frayed. He flicks the envelope against his leg to knock it into shape. Then he cocks his head as sounds ring out from behind a door half way along the corridor. He hears muffled voices, heavy laughter, a yelp of anger, a high-pitched chattering sound, more laughter ...

"Who's that?" Ruben asks.

Cole shakes his head. He doesn't know and he doesn't care.

"Come on, Rube," he says, as he moves towards the door. "Let's get this done."

Ruben follows him. His coat makes a faint clink as he walks.

At the door, Cole pauses for a moment. He's struck by a fleeting feeling that something's about to happen.

Beyond the door ... there's something beyond the door ... something waiting for him ... something that could be very good, or very bad. Or both. He doesn't know. It's just something, an unknown sense, a brief whisper in the back of his mind – *be careful* – and then it's gone.

Disappeared.

Never happened.

Never was.

Cole looks at the envelope in his hand, thinks about it for a second, then pushes open the glass door into the bar.

Ruben follows him.

The bar is a big rectangular room with a high ceiling and acres of grimy red carpet. It hasn't been cleaned from the night before and most of the tables are littered with the remains of a Saturday night – empty glasses, empty bottles, empty crisp packets. Rainy light filters in through a stained-glass window and dapples the walls and the wooden top of the bar with dark lights. The bar itself spans the whole back wall, a long greasy counter lined with bottles and beer pumps and glasses in racks. Behind the bar, a man in a grubby white shirt is leaning against the till, drinking whisky and smoking a cigarette.

When Cole and Ruben enter the bar, the man looks up and studies them with hungover eyes. He frowns for a moment and squints into the gloom, then he raises his hand in a lazy wave of recognition.

Cole nods back, and holds up the envelope.

The man grins and tips his glass.

"Roy English," Ruben whispers to his brother. "I don't like him."

"No one likes him," says Cole.

"He's a snake," Ruben says.

"This is business."

Cole looks around the bar. Across the room, three men are sitting at a table with their backs against the wall. Two of them are fairly old – late 40s, early 50s – but they both look like they can handle themselves. One of them is completely bald, with a long nose, wire-rimmed glasses and strange, pinkish eyes. The other one has slicked grey hair and hooded eyes and battle scars on his face like an old boxer. They're both wearing suits, and they're both wearing the dead look of men who always get what they want and don't care how they get it.

The third man is younger – mid-20s, maybe. Lean and hard, with waxy skin and short black hair. He's dressed in a dark suit, black T-shirt and sunglasses. Cole thinks he looks like a gunslinger.

A slim young girl dressed in blue joggers and a short blue T-shirt is standing with her back to Cole in front of the three men. She's pointing at the table, waving her hand in anger, arguing about something

Apart from that, the place is empty.

It doesn't feel right to Cole. He knows these places, and he knows they never feel right, but his instinct tells him there's something else going on here.

There's some kind of edge in the air, something about to happen.

He can feel it in his bones.

A raised voice interrupts his thoughts – "Hey, get off, I *told* you ..." – and his eyes are drawn again to the table by the wall. The girl is glaring down at the gunslinger, hissing at him in fury, jabbing her finger at his face.

"If you touch me again ..." she snaps.

The man laughs and raises his hands in mock surrender.

"I'll kill you," the girl says.

"Ooohhh! You scaring me."

The gunslinger's voice is soft but hard, his words drawn out and marked with a strong foreign accent. A cruel grin plays on his lips as he glances across at his two companions and mouths something to them. They nod and look at the girl like butchers looking at meat.

Cole knows what kind of men they are. He knows what they do. And he doesn't much care. But the girl ... there's something about the girl that moves him ... something familiar ... like the sound of a voice in a drifting wind. He doesn't know what it is. He's fairly sure he's never seen her before, but it's hard to tell. She still has her back to him, so he can't see her face, just the back of her head, her neck, the shape of her body ... her skin.

God ... her skin.

She's wearing her joggers low on her hips and her T-shirt high on her middle, which reveals a flash of bare skin and white cotton that's hot enough to tear a hole in Cole's heart. But that isn't it ... not *all* of it, anyway. That's just body stuff – solid, uncomplicated, simple. No, what really moves him about the girl is something else altogether ... something he can't put a finger on ... something about the way she stands, the way she moves, her unseen smile.

Pictures.

That's what it is – pictures.

She stirs pictures in his mind.

Just then, Roy English's voice calls out from behind the bar. "Hey, Cole – you waiting for a bus there or what?"

Cole looks over at him.

Roy takes a pull on his cigarette and waves Cole over.

Cole looks across at the three men and the girl again. One of the older men, the bald one, has something in his lap. It's some kind of box or small crate, and the girl is leaning across the table to try to grab it from him. As she leans over, the gunslinger grins and grabs her backside in a rough grip. The girl yelps and straightens up, lashing out at him, but he leans back in his seat and avoids the slap with ease. The girl swears at him. More laughter rings out.

'It's nothing to do with us,' Cole tells himself. 'Whatever it is, whoever she is … it's nothing to do with us.'

He looks at his brother, nods, and they head across to the bar.

CHAPTER 3
MONKEY BUSINESS

Roy English watches the Ford brothers as they approach the bar, and hides his thoughts behind a vacant smile.

'Look at them,' he thinks. 'Christ, will you look at them? What are they like? I mean, the runty one with the weird eyes ... he ain't right in the head, is he? Never was. Anyone can see that. I mean, look at him. Jesus!'

Roy angles his head for a better look, and he notices how Ruben's features seem to shift in the light. He shudders. It's disturbing. But kind of funny, too. And then the light seems to change again, like a clouded moon, and for a moment Ruben looks like something from another time. A time when beggar boys roamed the night with long knives and blackjacks and raw leather sacks, and packs of dogs ran the streets looking for flesh-caked rags ...

And that isn't quite so funny.

Roy doesn't want to think about that.

He shakes the pictures from his head and turns his mind to Cole. He tries to remember the last time he'd seen him.

'It wasn't that long ago, was it?' he asks himself. 'A year, maybe eighteen months? But, God, he's grown. Jesus! Look at him. How old is he now? He can't be much more than sixteen or seventeen, if that, but he ain't no kid any more. Look at the size of him. He's nearly as big as his father. Nearly as scary, too. The way he looks at you, like you don't exist, like you ain't much more than a dirty little bug ...'

Roy English doesn't want to think about that either.

"All right, boys?" he says as Cole and Ruben reach the bar. "How's it going?"

Cole puts the envelope on the counter.

Roy grins. "You want a drink? Get you a beer? No? How about you, young Ruben? You want a Coke or something?"

Ruben looks at Cole.

Cole shakes his head and slides the envelope across the bar. "V5C, MOT, full service history," he says.

"V-what?" says Roy.

"V5C, the vehicle registration document ... the log book. You wanted a log book, didn't you?"

"Yeah, right."

"It's all there," Cole says. "You want to check it?"

Roy shakes his head. "I trust you."

Cole shrugs. He knows Roy doesn't trust him. Roy English doesn't trust anyone. The only reason he doesn't want to check the contents of the envelope is to avoid any chance of causing offence. Not to Cole personally, but through him, to his father. Because, like most people, Roy English is shit-scared of Baby-John Ford. Even now, with Baby-John locked up in prison – and not likely to get out for years – Roy's still terrified of Baby-John. He'd never admit it, of course. He dresses up his fear as respect, or regard, or even friendship. But it's fear all right. Stone-cold fear.

Not that Cole cares.

Fear? Respect? Offence?

He can take it or leave it.

Roy goes over to the till, digs around in the drawer, then goes back to the bar and places three £20 notes on the counter.

Cole looks at the notes, then at Roy. "What's that?"

"Sixty quid … that's what Joe said. Sixty for the log book –"

"It's a hundred," Cole says.

"No … hold on –" Roy begins.

"It's a hundred," Cole repeats.

"You sure?"

Cole just stares at him.

Roy thinks about it for a moment. He wonders if it's worth trying to push it, but the look in Cole's eyes tells him it isn't.

"Oh, yeah," he says with a grin. "Yeah, that's right. I forgot about the MOT. That's what it was – sixty quid for the service and the log book, and then another forty –"

A crash of breaking glass stops him dead and he looks over at the three men and the girl.

"Shit!" he hisses through his teeth. "What the hell are they doing now?"

Cole looks round.

The girl has moved to the side of the table and she's wrestling with one of the older men, the one with the scars on his face. She's standing over him, yelling in his face and trying to hit him. But he has hold of her wrists, so all she can do is swing her arms around over the table, knocking over bottles and glasses. The other two men are looking on with smiles on their faces.

Now that she no longer has her back to him, Cole can see her face.

Her face.

The dark almond eyes ... the lips, the cheeks, the pale skin ... the long braided hair, sculpted to her head, like patterned ropes of chestnut silk ...

"Rachel," Ruben whispers.

Cole gives his brother a sharp look. "What did you say?"

"She looks like –"

"No, she doesn't. She doesn't look like anyone."

Ruben blinks, taken aback by the tone of Cole's voice.

Cole touches his brother's face. "Hey, Rube, I'm sorry. I didn't mean –"

"It's a monkey," Ruben says.

"What?"

Ruben points at the table. "A monkey."

Cole looks across the room. Scar Face has let go of the girl's wrists and she's moved away from the men. She's sitting on a chair to one side, staring at something on the table. The three men have cleared the broken glass from the table, carelessly sweeping it to the floor, and started their smoking and drinking again.

Now that Cole has a clear view of the table, he can see what the girl's looking at. He can see it, but he can't quite believe it. He blinks a couple of times, frowns and looks again, just to make sure. But there's no mistake. A small brown monkey is sitting on the table in front of the three men. It's wearing a nappy, and it's bobbing its head up and down and holding a lit cigarette, not exactly sure what to do with it.

"What the hell ...?" says Cole. "What's that?"

"It's a monkey," Ruben replies.

"I know it's a *monkey* – what's it doing in here? What's it doing with *them*?"

"Doing bad," says Ruben.

Over at the table, the monkey throws the cigarette to the floor. The bald man picks it up and pushes it back at the monkey. The monkey bares its teeth and chatters at the bald man. It makes a high-pitched noise like a bird – *chicka-chicka-chicka-chicka ... eee-eee-eee!* The bald man swears and swings his hand at the monkey, and then he laughs as it jumps off the table and scuttles under a chair.

"He got some balls," the bald man says. "I give you that, he got some balls."

Scar Face pulls on a long leather lead to drag the monkey out from under the chair.

"He's a she," he says. "You watch it, mind, the little bitch can bite." He looks over at the girl. "Just like this one."

The bald man grins and turns to the gunslinger sitting beside him. "Hey, Jordi," he says, and he punches his arm. "You think we can use a little bitch like that?"

"The monkey or the girl?" says Jordi.

"Either ... both ... what you think?"

"Don't matter to me," Jordi answers. His voice is soft as he eyes the girl. "They all the same in the end."

CHAPTER 4
THE CAGE DOOR

The girl hasn't given up. She's just waiting, biding her time, working things out. She doesn't really know what she's doing now, or what she's going to do next. But one thing's for sure – whatever happens, however bad it gets, she isn't leaving without the monkey.

She watches in silence as Scar Face unties the lead from the monkey's collar. He threads it through a hole in the back of the pet carrier and ties it back onto the monkey's collar. Then he tugs hard on the lead, dragging the squealing monkey into the carrier. As soon as it's inside, the man shuts the cage door and slaps his hand hard on the top. The monkey goes quiet.

The girl shakes her head.

Scar Face drinks from his glass, wipes his mouth on the back of his hand, and turns to the bald man.

"So," he says, "you want it or not?"

The bald man waggles his hand – *maybe, maybe not* – and looks at the girl. She looks back at him. She swallows her anger and tries to stay calm, but the meanness in his eyes is too much for her and she has to look away.

She looks instead at the two boys standing at the bar. She'd seen them when they'd first come in, but she hadn't taken much notice of them at the time. She'd had other things on her mind. And, besides, they weren't anything to get excited about, were they? Just a couple of local boys, another two chancers looking out for themselves, doing their deals, same as everyone else.

But now, as she looks at them a bit harder, she sees she might have been wrong. Maybe they aren't quite the same as everyone else after all ... maybe they *are* different? The funny-looking short one, for instance, the younger one in the big black coat ... the way he's staring at the other boy, the intensity in his eyes, the purity.

'God,' she thinks, 'you'd think he was looking at the only living thing in the world.'

And she likes that.

She isn't sure why, but she likes it.

And the other one, the only-living-thing-in-the-world, the way he's staring at her ... the look on his face.

'Well, how about that?' she thinks. 'That's something, isn't it? That's not a look you come across every day.'

And she likes that too.

She looks back at him, gazes into his eyes, dares him to show himself.

'Show me what you are,' she thinks. 'Show me something. Go on. I dare you. What are you going to do? Are you going to help me? Or are you going to laugh at me, too? Or maybe you're just going to stand there all day and stare at my tits?'

The boy lowers his eyes.

'Sorry,' the girl thinks, 'I didn't mean … well, you know what I mean.'

She carries on staring at him, in the hope he'll raise his eyes again, in the hope she'll see his face. She knows it's wrong, that this is neither the time nor the place for those kinds of thoughts, but she can't help it. She never could. And, besides, he *is* pretty good to look at. Tallish … but not too tall. Good-looking … but not too good-looking.

Kind?

Maybe …

Maybe not.

It's hard to tell.

His face gives nothing away.

But at least he looks honest ... in a lawless kind of way. With his home-cut hair, his faded T-shirt, his nothing jeans and his nowhere jacket and his age-old dirt-white trainers.

'Help me,' she says to him in silence. 'For God's sake, do something to help me.'

CHAPTER 5
RACHEL'S GHOST

Cole can't look at the girl any more. He knows that if he keeps on looking at her he'll have to do something, and he doesn't want to do anything. He's tired of doing things. He's tired of everything. All he wants to do is take Roy English's money and go ... get back on the streets and go home. Get back to the yard, get back to work, forget all about it.

'All this,' he keeps telling himself, 'whatever it is, it's nothing to do with us. It's none of our business. These three men, these faces, these bandits ... whatever they are, whatever they're doing ... buying and selling, making the most of things … well, that's just the way it goes, isn't it? That's what happens. That's what they do, men like that. They buy things and sell things. Cars, drugs, booze, phones, cigarettes, monkeys, girls …'

'Like the man said,' he thinks, 'it's all the same in the end. It's all about money.'

Cole knows the girl is watching him, but he keeps his eyes focused on the three men.

He can guess what's happened, and what's going to happen. He can imagine the girl walking past the pub, maybe hearing the monkey's chatter, and stopping to look in the window. She was probably just interested at first, curious to see what was going on. But then she saw the men messing around, giving the monkey cigarettes, maybe drinks, having a laugh ... and that was too much for her.

She couldn't just stand there and let that happen, could she? No, that wouldn't be right. So she'd opened the door of the Live and Let Live and waltzed on in and told the men to stop what they were doing. She wouldn't have realised – or maybe she just forgot – that you *can't* stop these kinds of men. To them, cruelty is not a sin but a strength. And maybe she didn't realise, either, what these kinds of men are capable of, and how they could change her life.

Or maybe she *did* realise, but she just didn't care?

Not that it matters.

The man called Jordi is watching Cole now. He's staring hard, aware of Cole's close attention. The table has gone quiet. The other two men are watching Cole, too. Jordi has one hand tucked behind his back, like it's no big deal.

"You want something?" he calls across to Cole.

Cole ignores him and looks across at the front door. It's locked. Bolted on the inside, top and bottom.

Cole turns to the bar, picks up the money, and folds the notes into his pocket.

He jerks his thumb over his shoulder. "You know them?" he asks Roy.

Roy leans forward and speaks in a whisper. "The big one with the grey hair is Darnell Bliss. Your old man and your uncle would know him. Big name. The other two ...?" He shrugs. "I don't know. I ain't seen them before. I think they're Russian, maybe Albanian."

Cole says, "I thought Bliss worked up west."

"A lot of the old boys are moving out, expanding," Roy tells him. "You know, new places, fresh faces ... Bliss has got some buildings down by the canal."

"Is he still running girls?" Cole asks.

Roy shrugs again.

Cole says, "What's with the monkey?"

"I don't know."

"And the girl?"

"What about her?"

"Where's she from?"

Roy shakes his head. "Don't know, never seen her before. She just came in. Don't like Bliss having the monkey. Wants to take it off him." Roy grins. "You know, like return it to the *wild* or something."

"Are they looking at her?" Cole asks.

"For what?"

"Business."

"Maybe ... who knows?"

"You going to do anything about it?"

"Like what?"

Cole looks at him, just for the sake of it – he doesn't expect Roy to do anything.

Roy holds his gaze for a moment, then sniffs and moves to one side, leaving Cole looking at himself in a long silver mirror behind the bar. He doesn't like the look on his face. It's the look of someone who doesn't want to get involved but knows he's going to.

After a second or two, he turns round and gazes over at the girl again. Jordi's standing over her now, with his arms out, so she's trapped in her seat. Cole watches as he leans forward and whispers in her ear. She slaps his arm and kicks out at him. He laughs. The other two men are huddled together at the table, fiddling with something behind the pet carrier.

"Shit," Cole mutters to himself.

"It's her," Ruben says.

"What?"

"It's her ... Rachel's ghost."

"No, it's not," Cole tells him. "It's just a girl, OK?"

Ruben looks at him and grins his crooked grin as he waits for his next move. He knows his brother believes in ghosts, even if Cole won't admit it to himself. Ruben knows his brother's mind.

Across the room, Jordi stands up and heads for the toilets. He gives Cole a sideways glance as he strides across the floor. Cole looks back at him, checking him out in return. The way he walks, the way he dresses, the way he holds himself ... everything about him screams of pain and violence.

'Street laws,' Cole thinks to himself. 'The life ... tooth and claw ... whatever. The man's fair game.'

As Jordi goes into the toilets, Cole glances at the girl again. He wishes she'd just get up and leave, but he knows she won't. She can't. All she can do is sit there and try to look tough as the bald man goes over and sits down next to her and offers her a drink.

Cole takes a deep breath, lets it out slowly, and turns to his brother. "You got your tools on you?"

Ruben pats his coat. Metal chinks.

"Got any glue?"

Ruben frowns as he reaches inside his coat and rummages around in a multitude of pockets of various sizes.

After a while, he smiles in triumph and pulls out a tube of superglue. He passes it to Cole, and Cole slips it in his pocket.

"OK," he says. His voice is calm and he looks his brother in the eye. "Go and get a car and meet me in the alley out the back in ten minutes. Keep the engine running."

Ruben nods, looks across at the girl, then goes out the side door.

Cole takes another deep breath and stares at the floor. He needs to empty his mind. If he's going to do this, it's best not to think about it.

Just do it.

He puts his hands in his pockets and walks easily across the room. He doesn't look at anything in particular, just heads for the toilets as if he couldn't care less about anything. The door leads him into a damp-walled corridor. There's a bolted door at the far end of the corridor, and another door set in the wall about half way along. This one is marked *Gents*. Cole walks down the corridor and opens the toilet door.

Inside, Jordi is standing at the urinals, his back arched and his groin thrust forward. He grins with animal pride at the steaming yellow arc hissing into the porcelain.

If he heard the door open, he doesn't show it.

Cole doesn't stop to think. He just walks up to Jordi, grabs the back of his head and hammers his face into the wall. A dull crack rings out and Jordi goes down without a sound, dropping to the floor like a bag of cement. Cole shows no emotion as he looks down at him.

Jordi isn't moving. His eyes are closed. Blood flows from a gash in his head, his nose is broken, and his sunglasses lie smashed on the floor.

A moaning sigh bubbles in his throat.

Cole nods to himself, satisfied.

He isn't dead.

Cole stoops down and pulls a pistol from the back of Jordi's belt. It's a stubby little .22 calibre revolver. The grip is wound tight with black tape.

Cole checks the gun is loaded, then slips it in his jacket pocket. Next, he reaches under Jordi, feels inside his

jacket, and pulls out a wallet. Without
looking at it, he puts the wallet in
his pocket, then straightens up, looks
around, and goes back out to the bar.

CHAPTER 6
SHUT UP AND LISTEN

The girl's getting confused now. She doesn't understand the way things are going. First, the younger one comes over and pretends he wants to apologise, but all he does is crawl all over her, breathing his poxy words in her ear. Then, all of a sudden, he just walks off without a word. Next thing she knows, the creepy bald guy with the pink eyes is sitting down next to her. He offers her a drink, tells her he'll buy the monkey for her if she really wants it.

"I can get her, if you want," he says. "How much you think?"

"I don't want to *buy* her," she spits. "I just want to put her somewhere, somewhere she belongs ... somewhere nice ... somewhere wild ..."

The bald man shakes his head. "I get her for you ... you take her to the woods. Let her go." He grins, showing small white teeth. "Here, have a drink. We talk about it."

The girl pushes the glass away. "I don't want a drink –"

She stops and looks up as Cole comes back into the bar.

"Hey, Mister," he calls out, looking at the bald man. "Your friend got sick."

The bald man glares at Cole. "Eh?"

"Sick," Cole repeats. "He collapsed in the toilets."

The bald man looks at the man called Darnell Bliss and shrugs his shoulders. He's asking what to do.

Bliss looks over at Cole. "What are you talking about, boy?"

"The guy in the sunglasses ... I don't know, he just fainted or something," Cole says. "It's none of my business. I'm just letting you know, that's all."

Bliss sighs, then looks over at the bald man. "You'd best check it out, Skender."

The bald man, Skender, frowns. "Eh? Why? He'll be OK –"

"Just go and see."

Skender looks at the girl, then gets up and walks over to the door.

"All right," he says to Cole. "Where's Jordi? Show me."

Cole leads Skender to the toilets, opens the door, and steps aside to let him in. As Skender goes through the door, Cole draws the gun from his pocket and goes in after him. He shuts the door and puts the barrel of the gun to Skender's head.

"Don't make a sound," he tells him.

Skender doesn't even flinch. He stares down at Jordi. "What the hell? What's –?"

Cole jabs the pistol into Skender's head. "I said, don't make a sound. Do you understand?"

Skender starts to shake his head, then stops. He takes a breath, and nods.

"Move," Cole says, and he directs him over to the row of urinals against the wall.

Skender moves over to the wall.

"One step to your right," Cole tells him.

Skender moves sideways.

"Stop there."

Skender stops.

He's standing next to a metal pipe that runs along the urinal wall. Cole keeps the pistol aimed at him as he goes over to the pipe and gives it a yank to test its strength. It rattles a bit, but it's strong enough. It'll do. Cole wipes the pipe dry with the sleeve of his jacket. Then he takes the tube of superglue from his pocket and smears a layer on the pipe, just to the left of a bracket.

He puts the glue back in his pocket, then waits a few moments.

Skender frowns. "What are you doing?" he says. "What's all this –?"

"Shut up," Cole tells him. "Get hold of the pipe."

"What?"

Cole steps up to him and puts the pistol to his head. "One more word and I pull the trigger."

Skender nods.

"Now get hold of the pipe, both hands."

Skender does as he's told.

"No, not there ... there, where it's sticky. That's it. Hold it tight."

Skender holds the pipe.

Cole waits a minute, then he takes hold of Skender's right arm and gives it a sharp tug. Skender winces. His hands are stuck fast. Cole pats him down, looking for weapons, but he doesn't find anything. He takes Skender's wallet, puts it with Jordi's, then leans forward and speaks in Skender's ear.

"I'm out of here in five minutes," he tells him. "Keep your mouth shut till then. If I hear a sound from you I'll come back in and put a bullet in your brain. All right?"

Skender nods.

Cole turns round and goes back out to the bar again.

This time he doesn't stop at the door. He just walks straight over to Bliss and the girl, holding the pistol behind his back, and sits down at the table.

Bliss looks puzzled. "What do you want? Where's Skender? What's going on?"

"Shut up and listen," Cole says, and he jams the pistol into Bliss's thigh.

Bliss stares in disbelief at the gun, and his face seethes with anger. "What do you think you're doing?" he splutters. "Do you know who I *am*?"

Cole flicks the pistol so the barrel cracks into Bliss's knee.

Bliss swears, grimacing with pain.

Cole glances over at the bar and flashes a warning look at Roy English. Roy's scared, nervous. His eyes dart around the room as he wonders what to do or where to look. Cole keeps staring at him until he gets the message – *keep out of it* – and then he turns back to Bliss.

"Next time you open your mouth," he tells him. "I'll shoot your balls off, OK?"

Bliss nods.

Cole turns to the girl. "All right?"

She nods.

Cole gives her a brief smile, then gets back to business. He wipes the table with his sleeve, then takes the tube of superglue from his pocket and smears some on the clean surface.

"Hands," he says to Bliss.

Bliss lifts his hands, glaring at Cole.

"Flat on the table," Cole instructs him. "Just there."

Bliss places his hands in the glue. Cole reaches over and presses down hard on them. He waits a minute, then lets go, sits back and looks at Bliss. Cold rage is burning in Bliss's eyes, and Cole knows it means trouble. Bliss doesn't care about the girl or the monkey, he doesn't give a shit about them. He doesn't care about the other two either, Jordi and Skender.

The only thing Bliss cares about is himself. His name. His reputation. His standing. His pride. And getting glued

to a table and robbed of his monkey isn't
going to do his reputation much good,
is it? Darnell Bliss isn't going to forget
something like that in a hurry. And even
if he wanted to forget it, Cole knows
he can't. For a man in his position, for
a man with his reputation to uphold,
letting things lie isn't an option.

'Shit,' Cole thinks, 'I might as well
give up now. Shoot myself in the head,
save everyone the bother.'

As that thought echoes in his mind,
Cole stands up, reaches under the table,
picks up the pet carrier, and passes it to
the girl.

"We'd better get going," he tells her.
"That glue's not going to hold them for
ever."

She doesn't answer, just sits there looking into the pet carrier. Inside, the monkey makes a faint whistling noise. The girl smiles at the sound.

"Hey, baby," she whispers. "You're all right now."

"Come on," Cole says to her. "We have to go."

CHAPTER 7
HOT METAL

An animal has a living weight, a vitality, a life force that touches everything around it.

As the girl follows Cole along the corridor to the locked back door, the pet carrier swings in her grip and she can feel this life force in her hands. She can sense the monkey's weight, its fearful movements. They pass through the palm of her hand, making her fingers tingle, exciting her heart, reminding her of the simple thrills of childhood.

"You all right?" Cole asks her as he unlocks the back door.

She looks at him and nods.

He opens the door and looks out into the rain. A flicker of surprise flashes across his eyes, then he shakes his head and glances up and down the alley.

"This way," he says to the girl.

She follows him through the door and across the alley to a black Mercedes with tinted windows that's parked at an angle to the wall. The engine is running. Exhaust fumes are trailing from the back of the car, creeping along the ground like a bank of grey fog, filling the alley with the smell of hot metal.

As Cole approaches the Mercedes, the driver's door opens and a smiling Ruben gets out.

"What do you think?" he asks his brother. He looks with pride at the car. "Did I do all right?"

"Yeah, great," Cole says sarcastically. "An E-Class Merc. Nice. That won't draw any attention to us, will it?"

Ruben grins. "What?"

"Nothing ... it doesn't matter."

Cole looks over his shoulder at the pub to double-check that they're not being followed. Then he turns to the girl. She's holding up the pet carrier, looking at the monkey on the other side of the cage door. She's pouting and making soft clucking noises with her lips.

Cole says, "We need to go."

She turns to look at him. "OK."

Her voice, now she's not under threat, is sweet and alluring. The harsh London tones are softened by the faintest trace of another language, a language she grew up with and learned to forget.

Cole opens the passenger door. The girl gets in and rests the pet carrier on her lap. Ruben smiles at her for a moment, then he turns away and gets in the back of the car. Cole goes round to the driver's side. At the door, he takes the pistol from his pocket and wipes it with his sleeve, then drops it behind a pile of beer crates stacked against the wall. He doesn't like leaving it behind, but he knows he has to. Stealing a gangster's monkey and a top-of-the-range Mercedes is risky enough, but driving around in a stolen car with a loaded handgun in your pocket ...?

That's not risky, it's just stupid.

Cole gets in the car and shuts the door. He glances at the ignition. The dashboard is shattered and a twist of wires has been yanked out and shoved back in again.

Cole blinks, a small flicker of annoyance.

He looks at his brother in the rear-view mirror. "You hotwired it?" he says.

Ruben shrugs. "I didn't have much time. Couldn't find a key. But I patched it up. It doesn't look too bad, does it?"

"No, it's OK."

'Not that it matters,' Cole reminds himself. 'We're not going to sell it, are we? This isn't business. This is a way out, that's all. A drive home. Twenty minutes from now, this won't be a Mercedes. It won't even be a car. It'll be just another crushed-up cube of junk.'

He adjusts the driver's seat and gets ready to go. He does his best to ignore the eyes of the girl beside him as she watches him. Her gaze is silent and open, and it makes him feel awkward, almost embarrassed, and he isn't sure why. Cole doesn't like not knowing why. It bothers the hell out of him. But there's no time to dwell on it. So he puts it from his mind, shifts the car into gear, takes a final look at the back of the Live and Let Live, and drives away.

CHAPTER 8
THE BREAKER'S YARD

No one says anything for a while. The inside of the car hums as Cole drives steadily around the side streets. He doubles back now and then, drives in a circle once or twice, and all the time he's checking the rear-view mirror.

He's fairly sure they're not being followed – who's going to follow them? Bliss can't drive with his hands glued to a table. The two Russians, Albanians, whatever they are, are out of action for a while. And Roy English isn't going to do anything, is he?

'Still,' Cole thinks, 'better safe than sorry.'

After about ten minutes, he slows the car and takes a shortcut through an abandoned industrial estate, a barren complex of empty warehouses and burnt-out skips and acres of crumbled grey concrete. An open gate at the end of the estate leads them out onto a narrow track that runs along the docks. They keep going, and after another half a mile or so, Cole steers the car onto Canal Road, over the railway crossing, and then they're heading east towards the breaker's yard.

They're on their way home.

Cole turns to the girl.

She looks back at him. She's covering her mouth with the neck of her T-shirt.

"OK?" Cole says.

"Yeah," she replies, with a shy grin. "Thanks ... you know ..." She rests her hand on top of the pet carrier. "Thanks for what you did."

Cole nods. "I'm Cole Ford," he tells her. "And that's Ruben in the back. He's my brother."

"Hi," she says, flicking a look at Ruben. "I'm Trina."

Cole nods again, and this time he looks at Ruben in the rear-view mirror. His brother is hunched up in the middle of the seat, leaning forward as far as he can. His hands are clasped between his thighs and he has a look of happy expectation buzzing on his face.

Cole sighs and turns his focus back to the road.

He's really struggling with all this –
the girl, Trina, the way she keeps looking
at him, the way she makes him feel …
he's not used to it. He doesn't know what
to do. He can't think what to say.

"Where are we going?" Trina asks
him.

Cole breathes a sigh of relief. 'A
question,' he thinks to himself. 'I can
deal with a question.' He slows at a
junction to let a car pull out, then speeds
up again.

"Where do you want to go?" he says
to Trina.

She shrugs. She still has the neck
of her T-shirt pulled up over her mouth,
and Cole wonders if it's something she
always does, a nervous habit, or if it's
because of the situation she's in – alone

in a car with two strangers, two boys, not knowing where she's going ...

He says to her, "What were you doing back there, anyway? You know, in the pub, with the monkey and everything."

She shrugs again. "I don't know ... I was just ... I don't know." She shakes her head. "It's not right, is it? I mean, what those men were doing with the monkey. I hate that kind of thing. It makes me sick. So I just thought ... I don't know, I just thought I had to do something."

She removes the neck of her T-shirt from her mouth and starts to chew the tip of her thumb instead. Cole looks across at her. She smiles in an embarrassed way and plucks at a small gold cross on her necklace. After fiddling with it for a moment or two, she puts the cross in her mouth, between her lips. Her eyes seem unsettled. She turns and looks out of the side window.

"Where are we going?" she asks again.

Cole glances round at his brother. Ruben just grins and raises his eyebrows.

Cole sighs again.

Up ahead, a mobile snack van is parked in a layby. A couple of container lorries are parked near by. The drivers are lounging around the van, drinking from Styrofoam cups and smoking cigarettes. Cole flicks the indicator and pulls the Mercedes across the road into the layby. Gravel crunches under the tyres as he slows the car to a halt behind the lorries. He puts the handbrake on, but leaves the engine running.

"All right," he says, to no one in particular. "Let's get some coffee and talk about what we're going to do."

CHAPTER 9
INSIDE THE JUNGLE

Cole and Ruben and Trina sit in the car and sip at their too-hot black coffees. With the monkey chirping away in its carrier and the windows steamed up with the heat of the coffees, the inside of the car feels like a jungle.

"OK," Cole says, and he winds down the window to let out some steam. "It looks like we've got ourselves a monkey."

Trina nods.

Cole looks at her. "Any ideas?"

"About what?"

"The monkey. What are we going to do with it?"

"I don't know," she says. "I mean, I haven't really thought about it ..."

Cole nods and waits for her to go on, but she doesn't. He waits a bit longer, then he says to her, "You didn't have a plan when you were in the pub then? I mean, you weren't thinking of taking the monkey somewhere?"

"Where?"

"I don't know. I thought you might have had somewhere in mind."

"Not really. I just wanted to get her away from those men."

"Right," Cole says. He nods, sips his coffee, plays for time. He wipes some steam from the window with his hand. "Those men," he says, "the men in the pub … do you know anything about them?"

"They were just men," Trina says bitterly. "That's all anyone needs to know."

"OK," Cole says. "OK. Let's get back to the monkey."

"It's a capuchin," Ruben announces from the back seat.

"What?" Trina and Cole say at the same time.

Ruben leans forward between the front seats, and his eyes flick from side to side in excitement. "It's a brown capuchin monkey," he explains. "They live in South American rain forests." He lowers his head and peers into the pet carrier on Trina's knees. "I think this is a young one. It's not fully grown yet."

Trina looks at Cole with her eyebrows raised.

Cole shrugs. "He reads a lot ... remembers everything."

"I didn't read about it," Ruben says. "There was a documentary on TV. It was about this monkey place in Scotland."

Cole frowns. "You don't get monkeys in Scotland."

"No, they've got this place where they keep rescued monkeys," Ruben says. "Like circus monkeys and stuff ... pet chimps, all kinds." Ruben smiles as a soft trill comes from inside the pet carrier. "They've got capuchins there too," he goes on. "They rescue them. They take them off people who don't look after them properly and they put them in nice big spaces with trees and climbing frames and toys and everything. They like it there, the monkeys. It's good. They're happy." He looks into the pet carrier again, and his eyes sparkle. "They're just like him. They might be his brothers."

"He's a she," Trina says.

Ruben looks at her, and all of a sudden he seems embarrassed. He blushes, but then he looks at Cole with a wide smile, to let him know that it's OK, he's not suffering – it's a nice embarrassment. They hold each other's gaze for a moment, then Ruben puts his hand to the side of his face and sits back in his seat.

Cole smiles to himself, enjoying the moment. His brother doesn't usually say very much, especially around people he doesn't know. It's good to hear him talking so freely. It means he's comfortable.

And when Ruben's comfortable with someone, it means they're OK.

CHAPTER 10
SANCTUARY

"So, anyway," Cole says, as he finishes his coffee. "What next? Anyone got any ideas?"

Trina says nothing, just sits there tickling the door of the pet carrier with her finger.

Cole watches her. He's looking for the little things, the things that tell the story. Things like her finger nails, which are chewed to the quick. And the patchwork of cuts on the back of her hand, the scabbed welt on her arm, the phone number scrawled in faded biro on the inside of her wrist.

"We could go there," she says at last.

"Where?"

"The place in Scotland ... the one your brother knows. The monkey place. We could take the monkey there."

Cole blinks. "Scotland?"

"Yeah."

"You mean, drive all the way to *Scotland*?"

"Yeah."

He shakes his head. "Have you got any idea how *far* that is?"

"It can't be that far."

"What do you mean?"

She just shrugs.

Ruben leans forward again. "It's in a place called Crachan. The monkey place ... it's in a town called Crachan, near Oban, on the west coast of Scotland. It's about five hundred miles from here."

"Five hundred miles?" Cole says, and he shakes his head. "Is that all?"

Ruben nods, ignoring his brother's sarcasm and looking shyly at Trina. "It's called The Ape Sanctuary," he tells her. "That's wrong really, because apes are monkeys without tails. Or if they do have tails they're only short ones. Apes are chimps and gorillas and orang-utans and gibbons, the rest are monkeys. But it *is* a sanctuary, like a hiding place, somewhere to rest, so the name of it's not totally wrong."

Trina smiles at him, a little confused.

Cole says, "We're not going to Scotland."

"Why not?" Ruben demands.

"We're not going, Rube. That's the end of it, OK?"

Ruben's face goes blank.

Cole sighs. "All right, look," he starts to say, but then he stops.

A flashing blue light in the rear-view mirror has caught his eye.

"Shit," he says, as he watches the police car speed up the road behind them. He puts the car into gear almost without thinking and reaches for the handbrake, getting ready to speed away. But then he stops. It's already too late, he realises. The police car's too close. It's almost level with them now.

All Cole can do is sit there with his hands gripping the steering wheel and his eyes fixed on the approaching car. He's waiting for it to slow down ... his heart's beating hard ... he can't help fearing the worst ...

But the police car doesn't slow down.

It just shoots past in a blue-and-yellow blur. It speeds past the layby and races away up the road, getting smaller and smaller until it disappears around a distant corner.

Cole keeps watching for a while, just to make sure the police car isn't coming back. When he's happy that it isn't, his body relaxes and he loosens his grip on the steering wheel.

"We'd better get going," he says, with a look over his shoulder.

"You can drop me off at Bethnal Green," Trina tells him. "I'll get the Tube from there."

Cole looks at her. "Why? Where are you going?"

"What do *you* care?"

He stares at her. He's shocked by the tone of her voice – the sudden sharpness, the unexpected anger. Trina glares back at him for a second, and her almond eyes stab into his heart like knives. Then she turns away and stares out the window.

As she moves her head, a crescent moon of diamond studs in her ear catches the light. They glint like stars, and Cole is mesmerised by the shining jewels ... but then his mind clears and a low breath escapes from his lungs, almost a growl.

He puts his foot down, and the Mercedes screeches from the layby in a shower of dust and gravel.

CHAPTER 11
TORN-UP RAINBOWS

In the back of the car, Ruben crosses his legs and leans back in the seat, enjoying the comfort of the soft leather upholstery. Right now, his mind is split in two. One half is logical, thinking about practical things – Cole and Trina, the monkey, the men in the pub, how it all fits together, where it's going to lead, and what that could mean. But the other half of his mind isn't really thinking at all. It's drifting, floating, wondering ... imagining how it would be to rise up into the sky and look down on the car from above and see all the thoughts and feelings inside.

What would those thoughts and feelings look like?

What colour would they be?

What would they sound like?

Cole's thoughts and feelings would be red and jagged, Ruben imagines, with black lines around the edges, and maybe little shapes squirming around inside, like something you'd see under a microscope. Cole's thoughts would pulse like hearts, and they'd sound like thunder and lightning. Like electricity.

Trina's thoughts and feelings would have the colours and shapes of angry paintings, like torn-up rainbows fixed back together in the wrong order. They'd be jagged too, like Cole's, but not as hard, not as solid. They'd be jagged like splinters of wood. Cole's would be long and dark, like spikes of black iron.

'But listen,' Ruben tells himself, and he digs his thumb nail into the palm of his hand and listens.

The sound of Trina's thoughts are a thousand screaming voices at the bottom of a deep dark hole.

Ruben closes his eyes, and his mind goes blank.

Cole is thinking to himself, 'Don't get angry, don't get angry, don't get angry ... don't go there. Anger clouds things. Don't think. Don't think about the girl, Trina. She's just another moment, a passing face, someone to think about when you're old and grey. What? What's that supposed to mean? Christ. Just stop thinking, OK? Go home. Take Ruben home. Get him safe. Then … then …

Then what?

Then nothing.

Just go home.'

Trina is staring into the pet carrier, staring into the eyes of the monkey. It's sitting at the back with its tail curled around its legs and its small black hands scratching at its nappy.

'A nappy?' she thinks. 'For God's sake, how can anyone put a monkey in a nappy?'

The air in the pet carrier smells sweet and musty. A bit shitty, too, but not unpleasant. The monkey tilts its head to get a better view of Trina.

Trina moves her head in response and the monkey follows the movement. It's smaller than she thought. No more than a foot high. A small animal with a small round head. Its eyes are brown and strong, but confused, blinking and widening in the gloom. Its brown fur is dusty and dull, like the fur of a stuffed animal in a museum. Around its neck, the fur is almost bare, worn to the skin where the collar has rubbed.

Trina taps the door with a fingertip.

The monkey yawns, and she sees a small pink tongue, small white teeth, and two pairs of sharp white fangs. It closes its mouth and scratches its tail. Trina clucks her tongue, making a soft *tock tock* sound. The monkey replies with a series of low grunts.

Trina smiles.

She says to Cole, "I'm sorry. What I said just now ... that was a nasty thing to say. I didn't mean it. I was just being selfish. I'm sorry."

Cole looks at her. A warm glow balloons in his chest.

"Cole?" Ruben says.

"What?"

Ruben points through the windscreen. "Look."

CHAPTER 12
THE RAID

The wipers flick across the windscreen as Cole curses under his breath and slows the car to a halt. Trina looks at him. His eyes are set hard as he stares through the glass at the breaker's yard at the end of the street.

"What is it?" she asks. "Why have you stopped?"

When he doesn't answer, she looks out through the windscreen to see for herself. A sign above the gates of the yard says –

FORD & SONS – AUTO SPARES
Crashed Cars, Vans & HGVs,
MOT Failures, Insurance Write-offs
BOUGHT FOR CASH

The gates are open and the yard is full of police cars.

"What's going on?" Trina says. "What are we doing here?"

Cole doesn't look at her. "We live here," he says.

Trina stares at him for a moment, then looks at the yard again. Amid all the cranes and crushers and cluttered heaps of tyres, a small grey house stands alone in a patch of waste ground. It has a flat roof and water-stained walls, and a dirty white caravan is parked just behind it. A uniformed police officer stands guard at the door.

"You live there?" Trina says.

Cole doesn't answer. He's watching the activity in the yard. As far as he can tell, there are three patrol cars, a low loader, a tow truck, a Transit, and a couple of unmarked BMWs. About a dozen plain-clothes officers are poking around the yard – checking out the scrapped vehicles and piles of spare parts, searching the buildings – and a team of police mechanics are loading a matt black Lexus and a soft-top Audi TT onto the low loader.

"Can you see Mum or Uncle Joe anywhere?" Cole asks Ruben.

"They must be in the house."

Cole nods.

"What are the police doing here?" Trina says. "Are they looking for us?"

"No," Cole answers.

"What are they doing then?"

"They must be after Uncle Joe for something."

"Why?" Trina asks. "What's he done?"

Cole doesn't reply. He shifts the gearstick, looks over his shoulder, and starts to turn the car around.

"Call Manny," he tells Ruben. "See if he knows what's going on."

"OK."

Ruben takes a phone from his pocket and selects a number. Cole swings the car around, takes another look at the yard, then pulls away down the street.

Cole drives away from the breaker's yard, not sure where he's going, just driving, putting some distance between them and the yard. He's buying some time, trying to work out what to do.

'Get rid of the car,' he tells himself. 'That's the main thing. Get rid of the car, get rid of the girl, get rid of the damn monkey. Get your priorities right.'

Ruben leans over the seat and passes him the phone. "It's Manny," he says. "He wants to talk to you."

Cole changes gear, then takes the phone. "Manny?"

Yeah, where are you?

"Driving. What's going on? Have you heard from Mum or Joe?"

Yeah, Joe just called. The police raided the yard. They're taking him in for questioning. I'm on my way to the station now. Where are you?

"Is Mum OK?"

Yeah.

"Have they charged Joe yet?"

I don't know.

"What have they got on him?"

I don't know, Cole, I only just heard from him. I'll let you know after I've seen him. In the meantime, it's best if you make yourself scarce.

"Are they looking for me?"

Probably.

"OK ... look. Call me when you hear something, all right?"

Yeah.

Cole passes the phone back to Ruben.

Trina looks at Cole. "Who was that?"

"Our lawyer."

"Are you in trouble?"

Cole shrugs. "Where do you live?"

"Why?"

"Me and Ruben need to lie low for a bit. We've got to dump this car and get things sorted out. Tell me where you live and I'll drop you off."

"What about the monkey?" she asks.

Cole frowns. "I don't know … you'll have to take her home with you."

"I can't do that."

"Why not?"

Trina starts to chew the tip of her thumb again. "I ran away," she says.

"From home?"

"Sort of."

"What do you mean, sort of?"

"It's not a real home … it's *a* home. You know, a kids' home … like a place for kids with *problems*." She curls her lip in disgust. "I hate it there. It's horrible. I had to get out."

"So you ran away," Cole says.

Trina nods. "A couple of days ago." She looks at Cole. She's still nervous, still chewing her thumb, but there's a sense of resolve about her too. "I'm not going back," she says. "I'm never going back there. I'd rather die."

Cole understands there's no point arguing. "All right," he says. "But we've got to go somewhere. And we still need to work out what to do with the monkey. Maybe we could take it to the RSPCA or something, or maybe the zoo –"

"No," Trina says, with a firm shake of her head. "I'm not putting her in a zoo."

"Why not?"

"I hate zoos. They're like prisons. All those stupid people banging on the glass and pulling faces at the animals ..."

Cole frowns. "Ten minutes ago you were talking about taking her to this monkey place in Scotland."

"That's different."

"Why?"

"Because it's *different*. It's not a zoo ... it's not like a freak show, it's not a prison. It's a proper place, with trees and climbing frames and everything, like Ruben said."

"Ruben's never *been* there," Cole says.

"Neither have you."

"What's that got to do with it?"

"Nothing. I just ... I don't know. I just don't want her to be locked up in a cage, that's all. I know what it's like ..."

She pauses and lowers her eyes, and Cole thinks she's going to cry. But then she sniffs hard – swallowing her tears – and when she looks back up at him her eyes are strong and hard again.

"We're not taking her to the zoo, OK?" she says. "If you don't want to –"

"All right," Cole says. "I get it. No zoo."

"What?" Trina says, surprised.

"We won't take the monkey to the zoo."

"Really?"

"Yeah. Really." He looks at her. "That's what you want, isn't it?"

She smiles at him, a smile that takes his breath away, then she reaches across and touches him on the back of his hand.

"Thank you," she says.

Cole just nods, unable to speak.

Her touch is electric.

CHAPTER 13
ON THE ROAD

Ten minutes later, her touch is still there. The touch of her finger tips, the memory of it impressed in Cole's skin. Warm but cold – her touch ... he can't get it out of his mind.

As he drives, Cole keeps looking at the back of his hand, searching for the spot where she touched him. There's nothing there. Nothing to see, anyway. He wants to feel his hand, to feel it from the outside, but he's worried that touching it might remove the feeling inside, or that Trina might see him touching it and take his actions the wrong way ... not that there *is* a right way ... or a wrong way, come to that.

Cole doesn't know what to think.

In fact, he doesn't know what he thinks about anything any more. Things have changed. The *order* of things has changed. He doesn't know what he's feeling any more, either. Not about Trina, anyway. All he knows is that he can't stop thinking about her.

Ruben was right, of course – Trina *does* look like Rachel. She has the same fine angled face, the same soft dark eyes, the same radiant smile ... she could almost be Rachel's twin. And that bothers Cole. It bothers him a lot.

For one thing, he doesn't like to think that he did what he did, and that he's doing what he's doing – whatever that is – just because Trina reminds him of his sister. Because that doesn't make sense, and Cole hates things that don't make sense.

But that isn't the worst of it. That isn't the thing that bothers him most about Trina.

No, the worst of it is the way she makes him feel. He likes her. A lot. He likes the way she looks. Her face, her eyes, her lips, her skin ... everything about her excites him. She makes him feel good. She makes him hot. She makes him cold. She fires his blood and turns his body inside out. And that's fine ... it's a good feeling, full of energy, like a shot of pure adrenaline. And Cole wants it, he wants to enjoy the rush, the fire ... but he can't. How can he, when every time he looks at her, when every time he even *thinks* of looking at her, his mind shows him pictures of his dead sister?

How can he?

It isn't right.

It isn't *wrong* ... but it isn't right.

It's all mixed up in his head.

Cole drives on.

Thinking.

Thinking ... sinking slowly into the comforting hush of the car. The steady purr of the Mercedes' engine, the quiet clicks and chirps of the monkey, the low murmur of Ruben and Trina's voices ...

Time passes.

Ten minutes.

Twenty minutes.

Half an hour.

An hour.

"Cole?" Ruben says.

"Yeah?"

"We're on the M1."

"I know."

Ruben leans forward. "What are we doing on the M1?"

"Heading north," Cole says. "You wanted to go to Scotland, didn't you?"

Ruben grins. "Are we going to the monkey sanctuary?"

Cole looks at Trina. "Is that where you want to go?"

"Yeah," she says, and she smiles at him. "I mean, if that's OK with you."

Cole shrugs. "We've got to go somewhere. Scotland's as good a place as any."

It takes a moment for the meaning of Cole's words to sink in – a moment of dawning silence – and then Ruben whoops and claps his hands, and the monkey starts to hoot with excitement, and Trina turns round in her seat and beams at Ruben with a look of pure joy.

Cole drives on, his right hand on the wheel, his left hand resting on the gearstick.

After a few moments, he feels Trina's hand on his.

He looks at her.

She gives his hand a gentle squeeze.

"Thanks," she says.

He smiles.

The monkey's still hooting away, and now Ruben has joined in with her, throwing back his head and howling at the top of his voice.

"*Hoo-hoo-hoo! Hoo-hoo-hoo! Hoo-hoo-hoo!*"

Cole drives on, with Trina's hand still holding his.

Five hundred miles doesn't seem so far any more.

ABOUT KEVIN BROOKS

Kevin Brooks was born in Exeter and now lives in North Yorkshire with his wife Susan and a bunch of animals. Before he became a full-time author of hard-hitting, compelling teen fiction, Kevin did too many things to mention and lived in too many places to remember. He has been a rock star, worked in a zoo, a crematorium and a post office. Kevin's brilliant novels have won many awards, most notably the 2014 Carnegie Medal for *The Bunker Diary*.

'**Kevin Brooks just gets better and better**' *Sunday Telegraph*

'**A masterly writer**' *Mail on Sunday*

Praise for *Johnny Delgado: Private Detective*

'**The breathtaking pace of the end of the book brings it to an energetic conclusion, but it is the subtext of compassion, loyalty and justice which ultimately gives the book its resonance**' *Books for Keeps*

Praise for *The Bunker Diary*

'**An exceptional, brave book that pulls no punches and offers no comfortable ending**' *CILIP Carnegie Medal Judges*

KEVIN BROOKS has written lots of "compulsive, atmospheric" novels, including ...

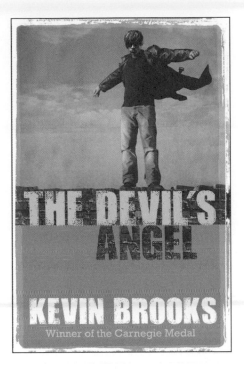

There was no fuss.
Dean just walked into the classroom.
Sat down.
Smiled.
Then beat another kid to a pulp.

It's half way into the summer term of Year 10
when Dean storms into Jack's life. Dean's scary,
but he's exciting too, and soon the two boys are
on course for a summer that will change their
lives for ever ...

Our books are tested
for children and young people by
children and young people.

Thanks to everyone who consulted on
a manuscript for their time and effort in
helping us to make our books better
for our readers.